31/10/22

30/1/23

D0892136

TRI

...last date
below:

00 1234049

01992 555506

...ibraries   Hertfordshire

This book belongs to:

....

....

To my lovely family, Grace, Katie, Zoë,
& especially Susan Krawitz – S.P.

Fear not spiders, Liliane! – R.G.

A TEMPLAR BOOK

First published in the UK in 2021 by Templar Books,
an imprint of Bonnier Books UK,
The Plaza, 535 King's Road, London, SW10 0SZ
Owned by Bonnier Books,
Sveavägen 56, Stockholm, Sweden
www.templarco.co.uk
www.bonnierbooks.co.uk

1 3 5 7 9 10 8 6 4 2

ISBN 978-1-78741-735-9

This book was typeset in Appereo Medium and Vampliers
The illustrations were created digitally.

Designed by Genevieve Webster
Edited by Joanna McInerney and Ruth Symons
Production by Emma Kidd

Printed in China

MIX
Paper from
responsible sources
FSC® C104723
FSC
www.fsc.org

DON'T LOOK AT IT! DON'T TOUCH IT!

Words by
STEVE PATSCHKE

Pictures by
ROLAND GARRIGUE

templar
books

One dark and scary **Halloween** night,
four friends named Sammy, Jenny, Sara
and Pete found a *strange* dark box.

Printed across the box, in big black letters,
were these words:

DON'T LOOK AT IT!
DON'T TOUCH IT!
DON'T OPEN IT!

"We'd better not **look** at it," said Sara.

"We'd better not **touch** it," said Jenny.

"We'd better not **open** it," added Sammy and Pete.

So **what** do you think they **did?**

They **looked** at it,

they **touched** it,

and then they **opened** the strange dark box.

And **what** do you think they **found?**

A *creepy* skeleton key,

on a rusty chain . . .

and with it was a **message**, which read:

DON'T TAKE FOUR STEPS! DON'T TURN RIGHT! DON'T FOLLOW THE TWISTING TRAIL!

So **what** do you think they did?

They took **four** steps, they turned right,

and then they followed the twisting trail . . . .

Soon they came to a **spooky** old house.

Across the door, in **big black letters**,
were painted these words:

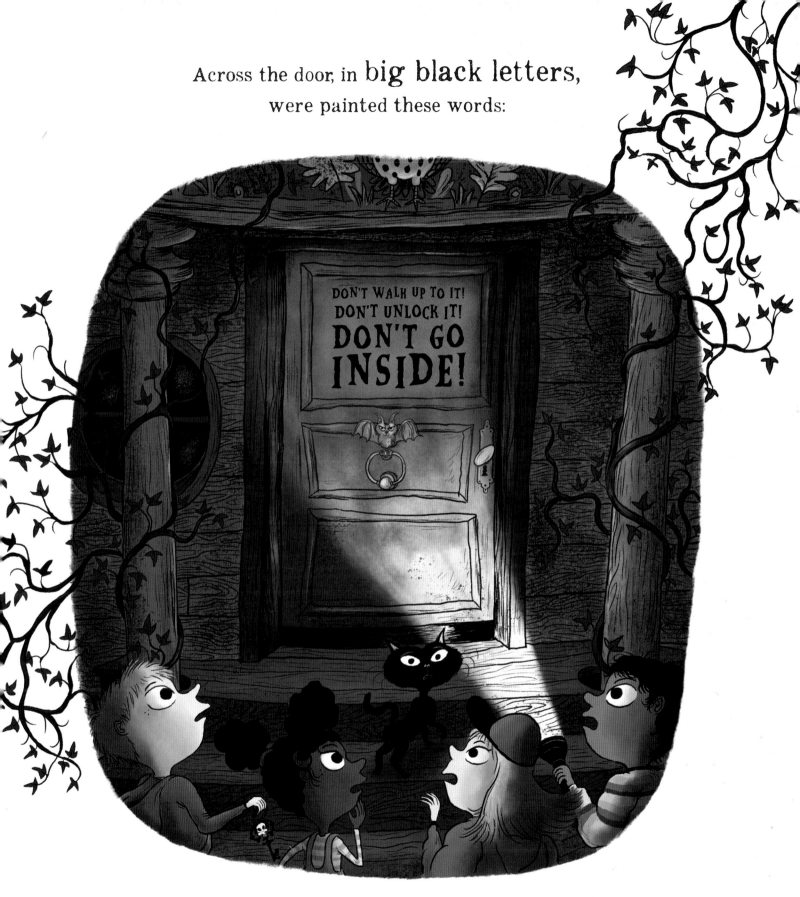

DON'T WALK UP TO IT!
DON'T UNLOCK IT!
DON'T GO
INSIDE!

So **what** do you think they **did?**

They **walked**
up to it,

they
unlocked it,

and then they **crept** inside the **spooky old house**.

Spider webs fell across their faces
like *witch's hair.*

"I'm scared,"
said Sara.

"Me too,"
said Sammy.

"Wait," said Sara. "I saw something move down that long, dark hallway."

And in a muffled voice the hall whispered:

"DON'T LISTEN TO IT! DON'T FOLLOW IT!

DON'T WALK DOWN THIS LONG DARK HALL!"

so what do you think they did?

They listened to it,

they **followed** it,

and then they **walked** down that long, dark hall.

Soon they reached some steep stairs leading to a black, cold cellar.
And from the black, cold cellar *strange* noises could be heard.

"Maybe that's
Jenny down there,"
said Sara.

"And maybe it's
not Jenny at all,"
said Pete.

But Sammy said nothing,

because now Sammy . . .

had disappeared too!

"No matter what we do," said Pete, "we're **not** going down these steep stairs, we're **not** stepping into that cold cellar, and we're **not** following *any* strange noises!"

so **what** do you think they **did**?

They went down the steep stairs,

they stepped into the cold cellar,

and they followed the strange, strange noises.

Soon they saw flickering candlelight coming
from beneath a small doorway. On the doorway,
in **big black letters**, were posted these words:

"What should we do?"
Sara asked Pete.

But Pete did not answer.

DON'T DO IT!
DON'T DO IT!
DON'T DARE
OPEN THIS
DOOR!

Guess why?

Because now Pete had somehow **disappeared** too . . .
and Sara was all alone.

so **what** do you think she **did?**

Slowly
she *crept*
to the door.

Slowly
she *pushed*
it open.

Slowly
she *peeked*
inside.

And **what** do you think she **saw**?

SURPRISE!

All of her friends, including Sammy, Jenny and Pete, were throwing Sara a surprise **Halloween birthday party!**

TRICK OR TREAT?!

There were pumpkins, scary costumes
and punch. And above one corner
of a ghostly table there hung a sign.

What do you think it **said?**

More picture books from Templar:

ISBN: 978-1-78741-950-6

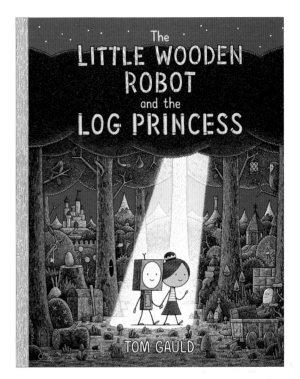

ISBN: 978-1-78741-917-9

ISBN: 978-1-78741-805-9

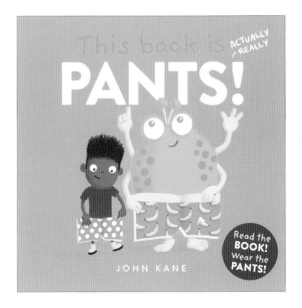

ISBN: 978-1-78741-923-0